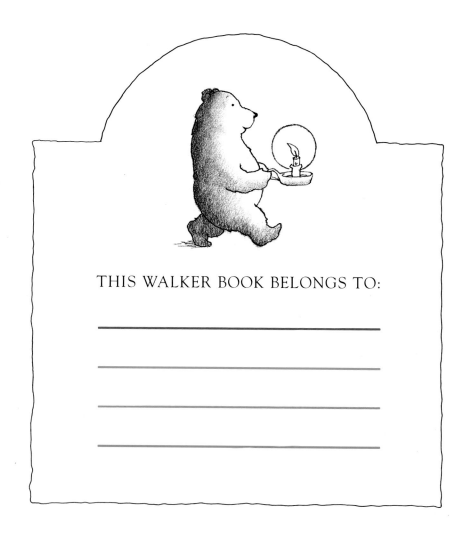

THIS WALKER BOOK BELONGS TO:

_____

_____

_____

_____

For Oscar

First published 1994 by
Walker Books Ltd
87 Vauxhall Walk
London SE11 5HJ

This edition published 1996

2 4 6 8 10 9 7 5 3

© 1994 Catherine and Laurence Anholt

This book has been typeset in Bembo.

Printed in Hong Kong

British Library Cataloguing in Publication Data
A catalogue record for this book is
available from the British Library.
ISBN 0-7445-4374-6

What Makes Me Happy?

Catherine and Laurence Anholt

WALKER BOOKS
AND SUBSIDIARIES
LONDON • BOSTON • SYDNEY

What makes me laugh?

tickly toes

a big red nose

being rude

silly food

acting crazy

my friend Maisie

What makes me cry?

wasps that sting

a fall from a swing

wobbly wheels

head over heels

What makes me bored?

Grown-ups…

moaning groaning eating meeting walking talking

feeding reading sitting knitting stopping shopping

What makes me pleased?

Look how much I've grown!

I can do it on my own!

What makes us jealous?

Her!

What makes me scared?

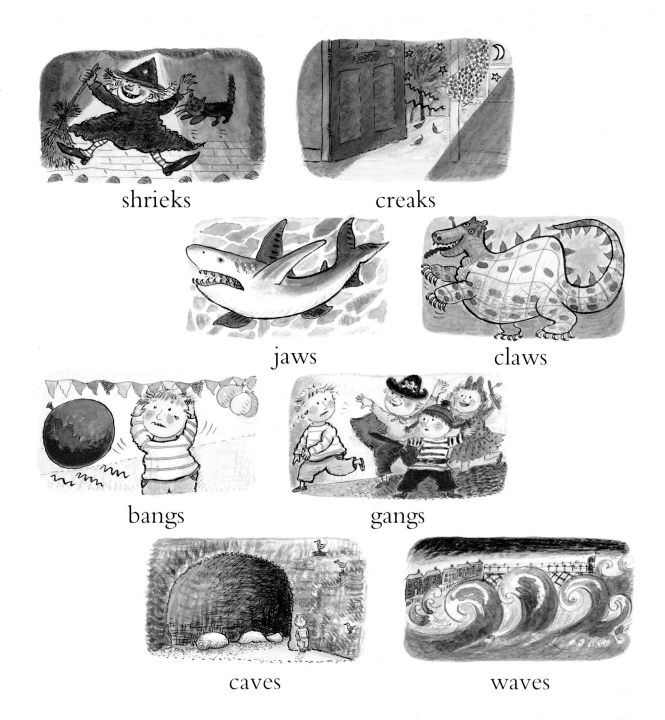

shrieks   creaks

jaws   claws

bangs   gangs

caves   waves

What makes me sad?

Rain, rain, every day.

No one wants to let me play.

Someone special's far away.

What makes us excited?

A roller-coaster ride

Here comes the bride!

The monster's on his way!

A party day

What makes me shy?

My first day

What makes me cross?

Days when buttons won't go straight
and I want to stay up late
and I hate what's on my plate...
Why won't anybody wait?

What makes us all happy?

making a castle

opening a parcel

singing a song

skipping along

windy weather

finding a feather and...

Being together.

MORE WALKER PAPERBACKS
For You to Enjoy

Also by Laurence and Catherine Anholt

WHAT I LIKE

"Children's likes and dislikes, as seen by six children
but with a universality which makes them appealing to all...
The scant, rhyming text is elegantly fleshed out by delicate
illustrations full of tiny details." *Children's Books of the Year*

0-7445-3019-9   £4.50

KIDS

"From the absurd to the ridiculous, from the real to the imaginary,
from the nasty to the charming, this is a book which touches on the important
aspects of life as experienced by the young child." *Books for Keeps*

0-7445-3011-3   £3.99

THE TWINS, TWO BY TWO

"A bedtime story about Noah's Ark captures the imagination
of twins Minnie and Max... All families will be able to relate
to this super book about bedtime with its large, simple text
and amusing illustrations. An irresistible end-of-the-day story
just right for reading together." *Practical Parenting*

0-7445-3142-X   £3.99

Walker Paperbacks are available from most booksellers, or by post from B.B.C.S., P.O. Box 941, Hull, North Humberside HU1 3YQ

24 hour telephone credit card line 01482 224626

To order, send: Title, author, ISBN number and price for each book ordered, your full name and address,
cheque or postal order payable to BBCS for the total amount and allow the following for postage and packing:
UK and BFPO: £1.00 for the first book, and 50p for each additional book to a maximum of £3.50.
Overseas and Eire: £2.00 for the first book, £1.00 for the second and 50p for each additional book.

Prices and availability are subject to change without notice.